MEERAS
FLOWERS

WRITTEN BY
AMY JIVANI

ILLUSTRATED BY
ANA OSEYNN

For Pink Ammachi

It was Friday afternoon at school, and Meera could hardly contain her excitement. She couldn't wait to get home and start helping her mom and dad with preparations for Saturday's Onam celebration. All of her family and friends would come together to celebrate what was known as South India's Harvest Festival.

When Meera's parents lived in India, they celebrated Onam for an entire week, but here in America, a full Saturday would have to do. Everyone would come over for delicious food, games, and of course, to admire the vibrant flowers that would be displayed on the entryway floor.

When school finally ended, Meera and her little brother Manu hurried home to their apartment in the city. As they ran up the stairs, an aroma of spices began to fill the air.

"Dad!" Manu yelled as they burst through the door. "Have you already started making the banana chips?"

"Well, hello to you too! And no, you're just in time!" he said.

Meera and Manu loved to watch as their father would cut the plantains into thin slices and then toss them into a pan of sizzling oil. They watched excitedly as the pieces would turn from pale beige to a glistening yellow.

Meera walked into the next room to find her mother sorting flower petals by color. Each year she would create a Pookalam (Poo-kah-lum), or colorful arrangement of flowers, to display on the floor. Meera always loved to help.

Mom went to the entryway and began to draw this year's detailed design with chalk.

"Why do we have to put so many flowers by our door every Onam?" asked Manu as he popped into the room, mouth full of banana chips. Mom continued to draw as she began the story Meera loved to hear every year.

"Once upon a time, King Mahabali (Mah-ha-bah-lee) ruled South India. He was wise and loved by all. Unfortunately, the gods grew jealous of this love and turned to the god Vishnu (Vish-noo) for help. Vishnu disguised himself and approached King Mahabali as a small boy. In an effort to welcome the boy, the King offered him food, cows, elephants, and even gold! But the boy replied, 'I only want one thing. Land!'

"Well, that's easy," responded King Mahabali. "How much land would you like?" "Only three steps worth," he replied. The King willingly agreed.

Suddenly, the small boy began to grow in size. He grew so much that he was now enormous! He took his first giant step covering all of the sky. He then took his second step covering all of the ground and everything underneath it. At this moment, King Mahabali realized that the boy was indeed the god Vishnu. In an act of respect and devotion, the King bowed as the third step was taken. Vishnu was impressed by the King's humility, so in return, offered him immortality and a chance to visit his kingdom each year during the harvest season. The Pookalam is our way of welcoming King Mahabali each year with the most beautiful and colorful designs."

She put the finishing touches on the design as she took two perfectly intact jasmine flowers and placed them in the middle.

"All done!" Mom said as Meera stood closer to get a better look. The petals and grass shavings created an elegant arrangement of green, orange, red, and yellow, all coming together to form a captivating design.

"How did you get so good at this?" Meera asked.

"My mom, your Ammachi, taught me how when I was a little girl," Mom replied.

Meera missed Ammachi. This would be the first Onam they would celebrate without her. Meera remembered in the past years how Ammachi would come stay the weekend to help decorate and cook for this special holiday. It was such a wonderful time.

"You missed a spot!" Manu said as he pointed to an area with an empty chalk design.

"That spot is for your sister!" said mom as she hugged Meera close. "When I was a little girl, Ammachi would always start a Pookalam for me to design with any flower of my choice. This year you are going to decorate one all by yourself!"

Meera couldn't believe it! She smiled and hugged her mom as she began to imagine all of the different colors and flowers she would use.

"Get your shoes!" said Mom, "Let's go to the flower shop across the street to get what you need!"

"Can I come too? I want to help!" Manu asked with delight.

"Of course you can!" Mom said as she started making her way down the stairs.

Meera had been to the flower shop plenty of times, but today it looked different. The flowers seemed to greet her with joy as their blooming colors and fragrant perfumes filled the room. She walked up and down the aisles, stopping to examine each bucket of flowers, knowing she just had to find the best petals for her very first Pookalam.

"It has to be perfect, just like Mom's Pookalam!" Meera thought. After a few aisles, Meera began to feel discouraged. She wanted the Pookalam to be just right, but she didn't know where to begin. She wanted to use pink flowers, but what shade of pink? The purple petals looked nice too, but were they the right shape? And what about yellow, would they match the other colors? As she looked around with frustration, the colors began to swirl around her.

"Meera, honey, are you okay?" Mom asked, breaking her daze. Meera looked down, embarrassed.

"I... I ...I just don't know where to start! How do I pick the right colors? What if I mess up? What if it isn't perfect?"

"Let's take a break. How about we take a little walk?" Mom said. They walked out of the store into the warm evening air. The sun was starting to set, and the street traffic was humming along. They walked in silence for a few minutes, listening to the cars passing by.

"Did you see the yellow petals I put on one side of the Pookalam?" asked mom. "Yes," replied Meera.

"Did you know that I chose that specific shade of yellow because it reminded me of the banana chips your dad makes for us every year? They're my favorite, and your dad knows it."

"Oh," said Meera.

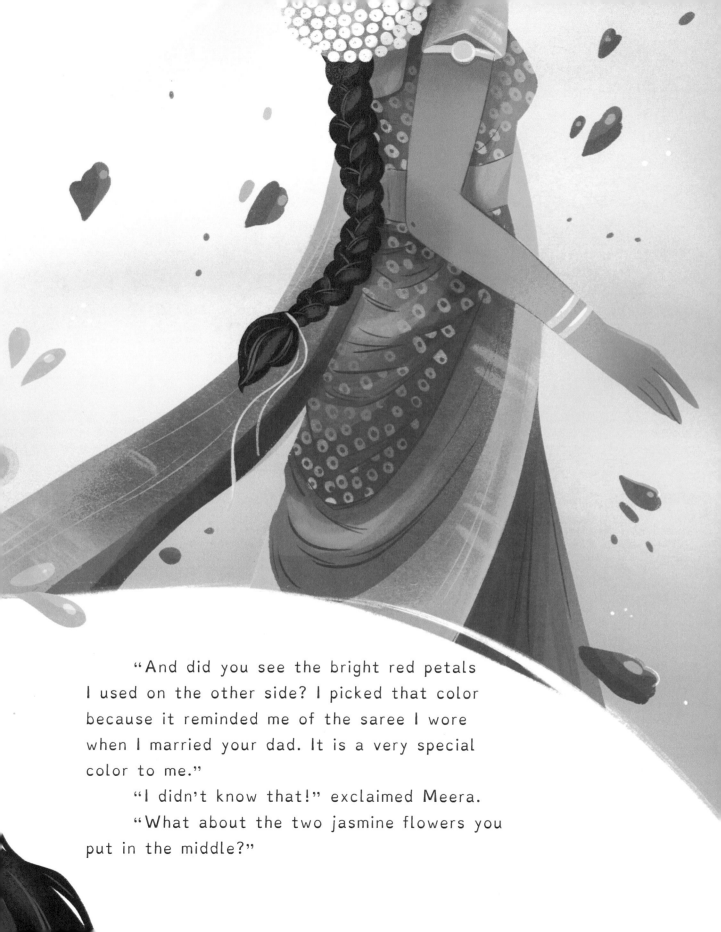

"And did you see the bright red petals
I used on the other side? I picked that color
because it reminded me of the saree I wore
when I married your dad. It is a very special
color to me."

"I didn't know that!" exclaimed Meera.

"What about the two jasmine flowers you
put in the middle?"

"Well, a jasmine shrub is known to be small but produces the most sweet-smelling little flowers. I consider both of you to be my sweet little jasmine flowers," Mom said as she hugged Meera and Manu close. They laughed.

"Wow...so every flower you chose reminds you of something?" asked Meera.

"Every single one!" said Mom as she glanced down at her watch. "Whoops, it's starting to get late and we still have much to do for tomorrow! What do you say we go home, sleep on it, and we'll come back to the flower shop early morning to get your flowers?"

"Sounds perfect," replied Meera.

That night when Meera was in bed, she kept thinking about what her mother had said about each color in the Pookalam and how each one was important to her in some way. She closed her eyes.

"I wonder what colors are special to me?" wondered Meera.

She began to remember Onam last year with Ammachi. She always wore a saree of the softest shade of pink with little flowers all along the edges. And every time Ammachi would visit, she would bring Meera little strawberry candies wrapped in bright red packaging. And the food, oh the food! Ammachi's cooking was the best!

The beige-colored Pappadam always so crisp and salty, the spicy red and orange Rasam so perfectly warm and soupy, the white, creamy Pachadi speckled with black mustard seeds...thinking about it made Meera's mouth water and also made her miss Ammachi even more. Suddenly she sat up in bed.

"That's it!" Meera thought. "I know exactly how to make the most perfect Pookalam."

Early the next morning Meera and Mom walked to the same flower shop.
This time, Meera was ready! She confidently walked each aisle,
frequently stopping to get exactly what she needed.

"All done!" Meera announced.

"Wow! So soon?" asked Mom. Meera nodded with a smile.

When they arrived home, Meera got to work right away. She used the chalk outline to carefully line and fill each part of the Pookalam. Her hands worked without stopping as if she were putting together a very familiar puzzle. As she finished, she carefully placed a pink and white lily in the middle of the design.

"There!" Meera said proudly as she looked over her work.

It was almost time for the rest of the family to come over. Meera rushed inside to get cleaned up and dressed. She picked out her favorite outfit for this yearly occasion. It was a long, flowing, cream-colored skirt and matching blouse lined with a shimmering gold that glittered when she walked. Meera knew this year would be different without Ammachi, but she was excited to see her family.

The doorbell rang, and soon their little apartment was full of laughing aunts and uncles as well as excited cousins running from room to room. The afternoon continued with games and stories, later followed by Mom and Meera's aunts performing a traditional folk dance as they did every year.

"Time to eat!" Mom called above the chatter. The table was beautifully laid out with the traditional Onam feast. Each place setting had a bright, green banana leaf to serve as a plate. A steaming mound of white rice along with different types of lentil and vegetable stews lined the bottom half of the leaf. The top half was arranged with some salt, different types of pickles, and dry vegetable curries. It looked absolutely delicious.

As everyone began to eat, Meera noticed Mom lean back in her chair. Mom watched as the family continued on laughing, talking, eating, and enjoying one another's company. Her eyes looked tired, but she smiled.

After the Onam feast, Mom and the aunts lounged on the couch laughing and talking while Dad and the uncles helped clean up. The children continued to play, only this time with a little less energy after such a big meal.

Soon it was evening, and everyone said their goodbyes. As Mom was about to close the door, she stopped and exclaimed from the doorway,

"Meera!" Meera ran to the door. "Your Pookalam! It's... It's stunning! I'm so sorry that I am just now seeing it!"

"That's okay, Mom. Do you like it?" Meera asked.

Mom nodded her head as she examined the petals more closely.

"Tell me about some of the colors you used."

"I was really missing Ammachi, so I thought of the many colors that reminded me of her," Meera said proudly.

"See the pink and white lily in the middle? It's just like the saree she always wore. And the red petals for the strawberry candies she would always bring, and the dark orange for the spicy rasam she would make, and..." Meera stopped. She looked up to see tears in Mom's eyes. "Mom, are you okay?" Meera asked with concern.

"Yes," Mom replied quietly. She smiled and hugged Meera close, "It's perfect."

Author Amy Jivani

Amy is an author and teacher living in Dallas, Texas.
She loves to read books and write stories for all
ages to enjoy. When she is not coming up with new
stories, she loves to spend time outdoors with her
husband and two sons.

Illustrator Ana Oseynn

Ana is a Belarusian illustrator living in Poland.
She's a big dreamer who talks to the world
through illustration. She loves spending time with
her family and friends, watching travel videos,
and exploring new places.

MacLaren-Cochrane Publishing, Inc.

Text©2021 Amy Jivani
Cover and Interior Art©2021 Ana Oseynn

Meera's Flowers Dyslexic Edition

MCPInfo@Maclaren-Cochranepublishing.com

Library of Congress Control Number: 2021942391

First Edition

ISBN
Hardcover: 978-1-64372-334-1
Softcover: 978-1-64372-331-0

For orders, visit

www.MCP-Store.com
www.maclaren-cochranepublishing.com
www.facebook.com/maclaren-cochranepublishing

What is Dyslexie Font?

Each letter is given its own identity making it easier for people with dyslexia to be more successful at reading.

The Dyslexie font:
1 Makes letters easier to distinguish
2 Offers more ease, regularity and joy in reading
3 Enables you to read with less effort
4 Gives your self-esteem a boost
5 Can be used anywhere, anytime and on (almost) every device
6 Does not require additional software or programs
7 Offers the simplest and most effective reading support

The Dyslexie font is specially designed for people with dyslexia, in order to make reading easier - and more fun. During the design process, all basic typography rules and standards were ignored. Readability and specific characteristics of dyslexia are used as guidelines for the design.

Graphic designer Christian Boer created a dyslexic-friendly font to make reading easier for people with dyslexia, like himself.

"Traditional fonts are designed solely from an aesthetic point of view," Boer writes on his website, "which means they often have characteristics that make characters difficult to recognize for people with dyslexia. Oftentimes, the letters of a word are confused, turned around or jumbled up because they look too similar."

Designed to make reading clearer and more enjoyable for people with dyslexia, Dyslexie uses heavy base lines, alternating stick and tail lengths, larger openings, and semicursive slants to ensure that each character has a unique and more easily recognizable form.

Our books are not just for children to enjoy, they are also for adults who have dyslexia who want the experience of reading to the children in their lives.

Learn more and get the font for your digital devices at www.dyslexiefont.com

Get books in Dyslexie Font at: www.mcp-store.com

5 I can read to myself   Complex plots, challenging vocabulary, and high-interest topics for the independent reader.

CPSIA information can be obtained
at www.ICGtesting.com
Printed in the USA
BVRC091607300821
R12567600003B/R125676PG615448BVX00006B/2

Time to Explore

Peepers Travel Adventures

By Vicky Hanson, Illustrated by Laura Tammisto

Dedication
*To many fond memories
of family vacations.*

I'm excited to travel,
With family and friends,
We arrive in Wisconsin,
Our fun never ends!

We see a state marker,
And as we've discussed,
With a hat shaped like cheese,
A photo's a must!

This lake is so pretty,
What would you do?
Would you want to catch,
A fish BIGGER than you?

Our tents are set up,
We've found the perfect
campsite,
Fireflies twinkle around us,
It's a perfect night.

We're feeling relaxed,
And warm by the fire,
Marshmallows roasting,
Soon we'll retire.

Visitor Center ahead!

So many pamphlets and brochures,

Many to choose from,

States to travel, and take tours.

The state we next visit,
Is so far away,
A jet plane will help us,
Get there TODAY!

The pilot announces,
This jet will go fast,
For your safety, stay buckled!
So many states we've just passed.

We've read our brochure,
It suggests what to see,
Niagara Falls is a must,
But it splashes on me!

Rushing water hits the rocks,
And it makes quite a spray,
But our raincoats and boots,
Keep us dry for the day.

Our next stop is Florida,
The Atlantic Ocean, so blue,
We pose for a picture.
There is so much to do.

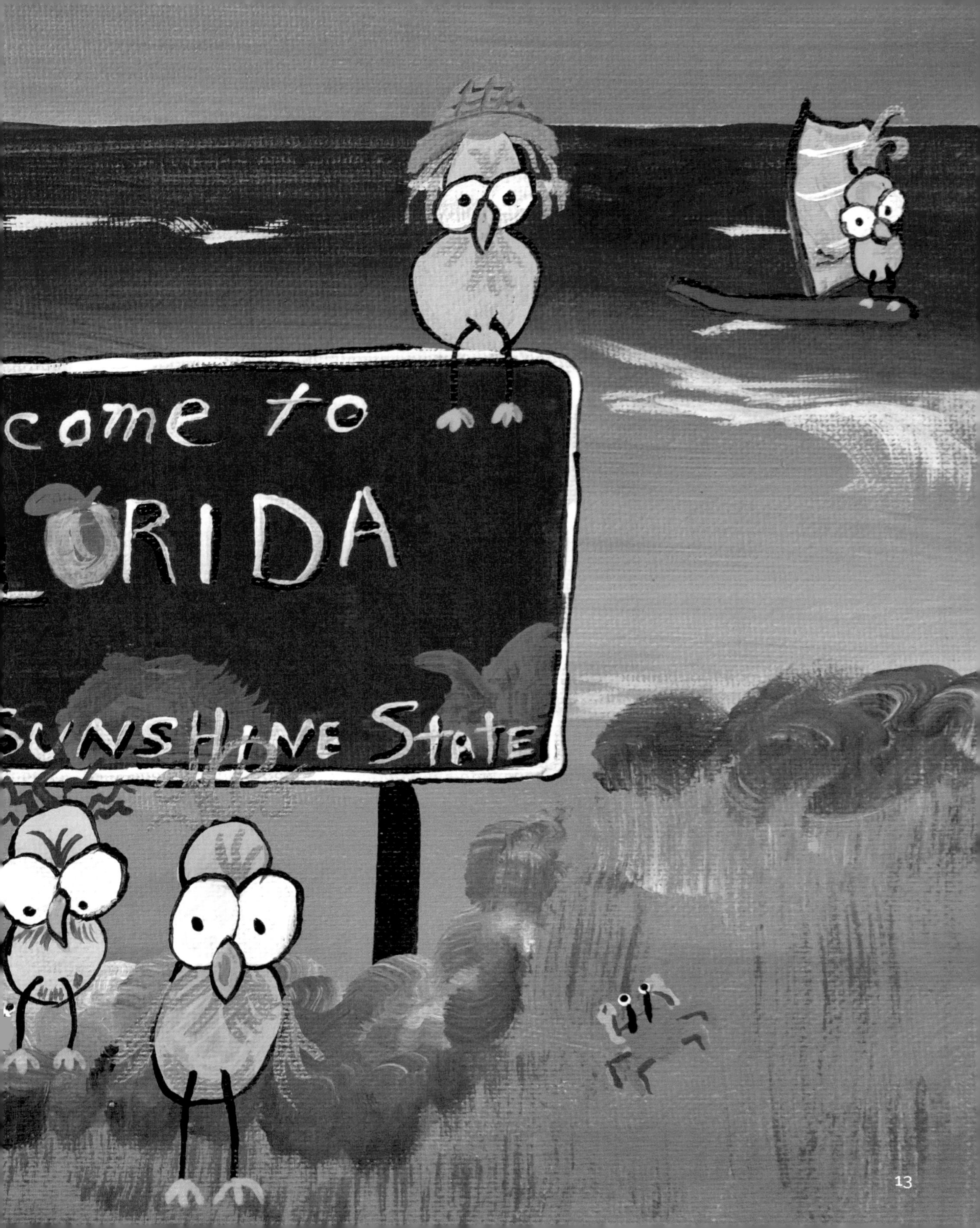
come to
RIDA
SUNSHINE State

We decide to go diving,
Under the water we go,
Scuba gear helps us breathe,
And see an underwater show.

Our journey continues,

And off we do fly,

But one of us chirps,

There's a restaurant nearby!

We decide that we'll stop,

And get some fresh fruit,

There's worms in the apples,

Oh, what a HOOT!

Our tummies are full,
To Arizona we fly,
We see the park entrance,
Let's give it a try!

We hike to the lookout,
The gorge is so deep,
We can't see to the bottom,
The drop off is steep.

We yell to our friends,
See the warning sign!
Stay away from the edge,
It's past the safe line!

We take a balloon ride,
A new way to fly,
Colorful rocks all below us,
As we glide through the sky.

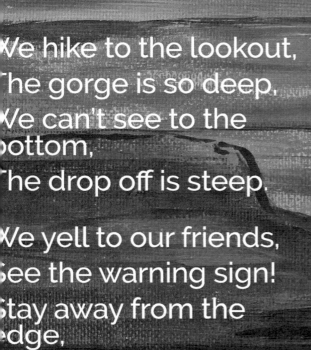

19

Do you see the state sign?
Do you know where we are?
We're somewhere out west,
We've come very far.

In Utah it's hot,
Very sunny and bright,
The sun makes me squint,
Sunglasses make it alright.

We're in Arches National Park,
Rock formations to view,
A tall arch ahead,
We can see straight through!

So glad that we've brought,
Lots of water to drink,
Very hot in this desert,
What do you think?

Utah has very high mountains,
There's still snow on the top,
A chance to cool down,
We'll rent skis at the shop.

We squeeze in the gondola,
To the mountain peak,
We ski down so fast,
Hope we don't fall on our beaks!

California, we've arrived!
Here's a great place to stop,
Golden Gate Bridge in the background,
A fun photo opp!

Giant Redwood trees,
So wide and so tall,
We can't see around them,
Or the tops, at all.

Our friends then decided,
Let's try a zip line,
My friends think they're fun,
But I think I'll decline!

Off to Wyoming we go,
To Yellowstone Park,
Buffalo roaming,
Glad we've arrived
before dark.

I have some binoculars,
To help me see far,
We've decided to hike,
Instead of taking the car.

26

Old Faithful is a geyser,
That shoots water so high,
It's called an eruption,
Water shoots to the sky.

We pose for a picture,
No time to discuss,
Oh no, we're too close.
It sprays all over us!

OLD
FaithFul

We don't want to go home yet,
Please, one more stop!
Sleeping Bear Dunes,
Another photo opp.

We're in Michigan now,
We're here to have fun,
One last adventure,
A hot day in the sun.

Do you know what a dune is?
It's a giant sand hill,
Can we reach the top?
Maybe we will!!

Hooray, we've made it!
A grueling climb,
We're just a bit tired,
It took us some time.

From here on the top,
Lake Michigan below,
In colors of turquoise,
A far away glow.

The most fun part of all,
Is racing downhill,
We try not to tumble,
Or take a spill.

29

We enjoyed all our travels,
We've been so far away,
Our forest feels good,
We're home now to stay.

The suitcases are heavy,
It's time to unpack,
Souvenirs bring back memories,
They help us think back

A cup and a cap,
To show where I've been,
And here is a pencil,
Let the collection begin!

Back in our neighborhood,
Our friends are ready to play.

We've missed one another,
We're home now, HOORAY!!

The swings in the backyard,
How high can we go?

Or a dip in our pool,
And a ball we can throw.

A new game to try,
What color ball should I choose?
We hit with a golf club,
I hope I don't lose.

A teeter-totter to keep busy,

While waiting our turn,

Do you like bean bag toss?

Is this hard to learn?

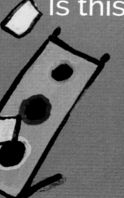

It's time to reflect,
On all the places we've been,
Time shared together,
Memories within!

Even though you can travel,
And feel free to roam,
In the end I still feel,
There's no place like home.

My story's not over,
For my friends and me,
Back to our jobs,
Which one would
you be?

About the Illustrator

With wings on her fingers and brushes in her hand, Laura Tammisto has become the "Bird Lady" in her fantasyland of characters. She laughs as she paints the birds in her stories, and sometimes they even talk back!

Laura has been in the design and decorative painting business most of her life, painting room-size murals for commercial and residential properties. Laura is an accomplished artist who creates fused glass creations as well.

A recent physical disability has caused her to reinvent herself. Painting her birds and illustrating picture books has become Laura's new passion. Her birdfeeders attract a variety of bird species from the marshland near her Portage, Wisconsin studio where she delights in their antics and imagines new adventures.

About the Author

Have you ever seen something so expressive and colorful that it just begged for a story to be written about it? Vicky Hanson's book *Peepers Gets Ready* is just that story, written in poetic form.

After seeing Laura Tammisto's bird paintings, Vicky and Laura decided to collaborate on their first book together. For Vicky, her poetry has always been a source of both comfort and fun. She writes poems to get over the tough times and enjoys more lyrical and spontaneous writing for humor and storytelling.

In this collaborative effort, *Peepers Gets Ready* came to life. The birds started to talk and to tell their own story. Their journey is full of fun and lessons.

Vicky and her husband live in the country near Portage, Wisconsin, where they are keepers of dogs and chickens and enjoy (and go broke) feeding the wild birds.